8-07

DALE EARNHARDT SR.

MATT CHRISTOPHER®

The #1 Sports Series for Kids

★ LEGENDS IN SPORTS ★

DALE EARNHARDT SR.

Text by Glenn Stout

LITTLE, BROWN AND COMPANY

New York ⚡ Boston

Little, Brown and Company

Hachette Book Group USA
1271 Avenue of the Americas, New York, NY 10020
Visit our Web site at www.lb-kids.com

www.mattchristopher.com

First Edition: April 2007

Matt Christopher® is a registered trademark of
Matt Christopher Royalties, Inc.

Text written by Glenn Stout

Library of Congress Cataloging-in-Publication Data

Christopher, Matt.
Dale Earnhardt Sr. / Matt Christopher.
p. cm. — (Legends in sports)
ISBN-13: 978-0-316-01114-3
ISBN-10: 0-316-01114-2
1. Earnhardt, Dale, 1951–2001 — Juvenile literature. 2. Automobile racing drivers — United States — Biography — Juvenile literature.
I. Title.
GV1032.E18C47 2005
796.72092—dc22

2006027897

10 9 8 7 6 5 4 3 2 1

COM-MO

Printed in the United States of America

DALE EARNHARDT SR.

Contents

Chapter One: February 18, 2001   1
The Last Lap

Chapter Two: 9
NASCAR

Chapter Three: 1951–1973   15
Starting Line

Chapter Four: 1973–1978   24
From the Back of the Pack

Chapter Five: 1979–1980   31
Champion

Chapter Six: 1981–1983   45
Checkered Flags

Chapter Seven: 1984–1997   53
The Intimidator

Chapter Eight: 1993–1998   66
Daytona and Other Dreams

Chapter Nine: 1999–2002   76
Finish Line Legacy

★ CHAPTER ONE ★
FEBRUARY 18, 2001

The Last Lap

He wasn't going to win the race, but Dale Earnhardt was still driving hard.

He steered his car along the straightaway toward turn four during the last lap of the Daytona 500 NASCAR stock car auto race on February 18, 2001. Earnhardt trailed the leaders. Ahead of him, Michael Waltrip and Dale Earnhardt's son, Dale Junior, powered toward the finish line, bumper to bumper, fighting for first place.

It had been a long, tough race. The Daytona 500 is the first race of the NASCAR season and also the biggest NASCAR race of the year. Already, the 2001 Daytona 500 had been one of the most exciting and memorable in history. More than 200,000 fans packed the grandstand and infield to watch the race on the 2.5-mile "tri-oval," a steeply banked track featuring three wide turns. Millions more tuned in on television. The lead had changed hands forty-nine times over the five-hundred-mile race, and even a spectacular eighteen-car crash twenty-five laps from the finish hadn't dampened anyone's spirits, for none of the drivers had been hurt seriously.

Dale Earnhardt was one of the most successful and popular drivers in NASCAR history. Since his first NASCAR race in 1975, he had won seventy-six races and earned more than $42 million. He had won seven driving championships and earned a reputation as one of NASCAR's best drivers, known for his never-say-die attitude and his aggressive driving.

Despite his fame in the race car circuit, Earnhardt never acted like a big shot. In an era when NASCAR was trying to be big time, he reminded everyone that NASCAR's roots stretched back to the days when drivers worked on their own cars in small garages and raced on weekends on small dirt tracks in the middle of nowhere. Like those predecessors, Earnhardt didn't race for the money but because he loved the sport.

At age forty-nine, Earnhardt's quick smile and hard driving style appealed both to longtime fans and to those who had recently discovered NASCAR. His black Chevy Lumina emblazoned with the number 3 was one of the most recognized cars on the racetrack.

Other NASCAR drivers looked up to him, not just for his success on the track but for the way he drove and lived. Earnhardt had started with nothing and built a NASCAR empire. He wasn't just a champion driver but also a car owner and a leader of the sport. He gave generously to charities and to his sport but refused to take credit for simply doing the right thing. As one driver put it, "Dale Earnhardt was what we were all trying to be on the racetrack and off the racetrack, too."

Although Dale Earnhardt had won Daytona before, as he entered the last lap, he realized this time he would lag behind. His car just wasn't running as fast as he liked. He decided to drop back from the lead pack and join the second group of six drivers.

Just because Dale Earnhardt was backing off didn't mean he had given up. He never did. He loved racing and always tried to do as well as he possibly could. He knew that a third-place finish would mark a good beginning to the season. A driver earns points toward the season title depending on where he finishes, so each place counts. Furthermore, by backing off he had decided to do everything possible to help Dale Junior and Waltrip, blocking other cars to prevent anyone from catching the leaders.

As he approached turn four, Earnhardt was going about 170 miles per hour. He hugged the inside lane, leading a knot of seven cars. Directly behind him was a row of three cars and behind them three more. Dale noticed another driver, Sterling Marlin, gaining on him from behind. He sensed that Marlin was about to try to edge past him on the right side.

As Marlin approached, Earnhardt turned his steering wheel ever so slightly to the right to close the gap and squeeze Marlin out. As he did, Marlin's car, still accelerating, tapped Dale's back bumper.

Such minor collisions happen all the time during NASCAR races. Cars travel at high speed in extremely close quarters. As they fight for position, they often bump and brush against each other. Few cars finish a race without a few small dents and scrapes.

Most of the time, these small bumps aren't a problem. NASCAR drivers are highly trained professionals and know how to prevent small collisions from turning into major accidents. Still, accidents are as much a part of racing as fouls are in basketball. Contact between two people trying to reach the same goal is inevitable.

But sometimes such contact can snowball out of control.

Earnhardt had just turned his wheel to the right when Marlin's car tapped him. With that nudge, Earnhardt's car began to slide sideways toward the concrete wall bordering the racetrack.

Earnhardt knew how to control such slides. Over the course of his career, he had been in dozens of accidents and hundreds of near misses. This time, however, something went wrong.

He may have been tired after racing 499 miles. His fatigue may have made his reaction just a little slower than normal. So many miles undoubtedly wore down his tires, making their grip on the hot track a little less sure.

Whatever the reason, Dale Earnhardt lost control of his car.

Instead of straightening, the Chevy kept turning sideways. Earnhardt slid past Marlin's car — and, still moving at well over 160 miles per hour, cut directly in front of another car running on the high side of the track.

Veteran NASCAR driver Ken Schrader didn't have time to react.

Bam!

Schrader's car buried itself in the passenger side of Earnhardt's Chevy. Locked together, the two cars hurtled toward the concrete wall. Earnhardt's car struck nose-first, then both cars careened along the wall, sending up showers of sparks and clouds of smoke.

Fortunately, the cars behind them were able to steer around the accident. Seconds later, Waltrip edged out Dale Junior to win the race. Race officials waved the checkered flag to signal a winner — then hurriedly began waving the yellow flag to warn other drivers of the accident.

As NASCAR accidents go, the collision didn't look that bad, especially compared to the eighteen-car crash that had happened earlier. That wreck had sent cars spinning in every direction and debris flying through the air. Several cars had been completely destroyed.

Yet despite all the damage, no one had been seriously injured in the earlier pileup, thanks in large part to NASCAR's regulations about safety equipment. Every driver wears a seatbelt and shoulder harness and is protected by special seats. A rollbar encases the cockpit so if the car turns upside down the roof cannot collapse on the driver. Drivers wear protective helmets to guard against head injuries and flameproof suits to protect them against fire. While accidents are common in NASCAR racing today, deaths are rare.

Each driver also has a two-way radio he uses to keep in touch with his team. After Earnhardt and Schrader's crash, Richard Childress, Earnhardt's team owner, immediately called Dale Senior. Earnhardt didn't respond.

Rescue vehicles raced from the infield toward the two cars. Ken Schrader was shaken up by the collision but otherwise was unhurt. He gestured to the rescuers that he was fine.

Two rescuers then approached Earnhardt's car, one from each side. They expected to find Earnhardt unhurt, although they knew they might have to help him get out of the crumpled car. Instead, they found him motionless, his head slumped to his chest.

The unthinkable had happened. When his car hit the wall, Earnhardt's head had whipped forward violently. He had fractured the base of his skull. Despite the best efforts of the rescuers, Earnhardt could not be saved.

Later that day, a NASCAR official made a brief announcement.

"We've lost Dale Earnhardt."

A NASCAR legend was gone.

⋆ CHAPTER TWO ⋆

NASCAR

The first American automobile race was held in Chicago in 1895. It may seem incredible today, but the fifty-four-mile race took nearly eight hours to complete. The winner, Frank Duryea, finished the race with an average speed of only seven and a half miles per hour.

Today there are many different kinds of auto racing. Racing is a major sport throughout the world worth billions of dollars. Due to the cost, most racing is now done professionally. Winning drivers earn prize money.

Formula One and Indy Car are the best-known forms of professional auto racing. Both styles feature very specialized cars that race for hundreds of miles on either closed road courses or tracks. Drag racing is also very popular. Two cars called dragsters race each other in a straight line over a quarter-mile distance.

Stock car racing is the most popular form of racing in the United States. The term "stock car" refers to a standard automobile produced by a car manufacturer.

Stock car racing began in the 1920s during an era of American history known as Prohibition, when it was illegal to produce or sell alcohol. But the law didn't stop people from procuring beer, whiskey, and other kinds of intoxicating beverages. Some smuggled it into the country from other nations, while others, known as bootleggers, made their own.

In the South, many people made their own whiskey to drink and sell. It was the job of government workers known as revenue agents to stop this illegal trade. Whiskey smugglers had to find ways to avoid these officials. Many tinkered with the engines of their cars to make them go faster so that they could outrun the revenue agents. Smugglers bragged to one another about the speed of their cars; to prove just how fast their cars were, some challenged others to races in front of their friends. These races were the first stock car races.

The races took place in cornfields, around horse-racing tracks at fairgrounds, and even on wide sandy beaches. They were very dangerous. Safety devices such as seat belts had yet to be invented and few drivers were very concerned about their own safety. They simply enjoyed the thrill of racing at high speed and the bragging rights that came with victory. Occasionally they'd even earn a bit of money from contributions made by drivers entered in the race, spectators who wanted to make the race more interesting, and local businesses that chose to sponsor the race. Any money a driver earned was usually spent on making his automobile even faster.

While Prohibition was eventually repealed, ending the need for fast cars to smuggle whiskey, stock car racing continued to grow in popularity. In 1946, a driver named Bill France decided to organize stock car racing into a sport and formed the National Championship circuit. Then, in 1947, in Daytona Beach, Florida, he created the National Association for Stock Car Auto Racing, or NASCAR. In 1948, he held the first official NASCAR race in Daytona on a track temporarily carved out of the wide sand beach.

Ever so slowly, NASCAR expanded, and in a few

years there were a number of cities in the South with oval dirt tracks made for stock car racing. Spectators paid admission to the races, and auto dealers, parts manufacturers, and others began to sponsor cars, helping drivers build faster cars. The best drivers began to earn significant money.

In the early days, NASCAR racing was wild and dangerous. Drivers did anything possible to win, bumping each other off the track, sabotaging each other's cars, and making modifications — often unsafe ones — to their own cars to make them go faster. Fans didn't mind. They loved it.

But it was after the first asphalt track was built in Darlington, South Carolina, in 1950 that NASCAR truly took off. Asphalt tracks were made with banked turns that allowed greater speed, and greater speed increased the popularity of the races. Over the next decade, more asphalt tracks were built, making dirt tracks a thing of the past.

Car manufacturers like Ford and Dodge took notice of the large crowds and realized that if one of their cars won a stock car race, fans were more likely to buy that model for themselves. They began to sponsor the best drivers, like Junior Johnson, Lee

Petty, and Fireball Roberts, paying them to drive a particular car model and even providing the car. Car parts manufacturers and oil companies soon began doing the same thing, and before long it was unusual to see a stock car without the logos of various companies plastered on its exterior.

The cars' engines changed, too, becoming more powerful and requiring specialized fuel. The tires were made specifically for the grueling conditions of racing over long distances on hot asphalt. In fact, other than its standard body, very little about a stock car used in racing is like the automobile driven by the average driver.

By the 1960s, NASCAR was beginning to shed its outlaw past. It was so popular in the South that by 1965 it was the second most popular spectator sport in the country, behind horse racing. Television took notice and began to air select races. Cars regularly went more than 100 miles per hour, and those who could handle the speed and intensity, such as Lee Petty's son Richard, became wealthy men. They employed their own teams, with mechanics who built the cars and worked on them between races, and their own pit crews to change tires, make minor repairs, and fuel the cars during a race. NASCAR was becoming a big business.

It became even bigger in 1971 when a tobacco company decided to sponsor NASCAR. They set the schedule of thirty-one races and instituted a point system to determine a yearly champion. Over the next decade, NASCAR began to spread across the country. Tracks were built from New Hampshire to California. In the 1980s, sponsors looked at attendance figures, realized the NASCAR audience was huge, and began to put significant money into the sport. Each year the sport became more and more popular, and by the 1990s, the best drivers were household names, as well known as any baseball or basketball star.

One of those names was Dale Earnhardt.

Starting Line

Dale Earnhardt was born to be a race car driver. His career mirrored the rise of the sport he loved.

Dale's father, Ralph Earnhardt, was a stock car racing pioneer. As a young man, he worked in a textile mill in Kannapolis, North Carolina, a small town in the foothills of the Appalachian Mountains. Kannapolis was the kind of place where everybody knew everybody else. It wasn't a wealthy community, but it was close-knit and neighbors helped each other.

Everyone knew Ralph, and everyone knew that what Ralph really wanted to do was race cars. He liked going to local stock car races and tinkering with car engines in his garage. He started racing, but with a growing young family, he couldn't afford to go into racing full-time. Instead, like many other race car driver wannabes, he held a regular job during the week, worked on his car at night, and raced on the weekends.

Ralph Dale Earnhardt was born on April 29, 1951, one of five children. When he was old enough, little Dale took to following Ralph out to the garage whenever he could. He loved everything about the place. The cars and their engines looked huge. There were tools and parts everywhere, an endless source of interest to the young boy. The garage smelled of grease and gasoline. He could get dirty there and not get yelled at.

Whenever his mother, Martha, couldn't find him, she knew where to look. He was always out in the garage with Ralph, his brothers Randy and Danny, and his sisters Kaye and Kathy, messing around.

On the weekends, Dale and his family went to watch his father race. Ralph drove in the Sportsman division of NASCAR, a series of smaller, shorter races, sort of like the minor leagues of NASCAR. Although he eventually turned to racing full-time, he never tried to become a full-fledged NASCAR driver. That would have meant traveling constantly, and he wouldn't leave Martha and the children for long periods of time.

Ralph earned a reputation as a top-notch mechanic and a fine driver. Other drivers would show up at the track with their cars and work on them right up until race time, but Ralph always arrived with a car that was fully prepared. While other drivers worked, Ralph just stood back and watched and learned.

When he decided to go into racing full-time, he promised Martha he would always make sure he was there for his family. Both had seen other racers nearly abandon their loved ones; neither of them wanted that for their family.

As a result, Ralph rarely traveled very far to race, usually competing on tracks in North Carolina or Georgia. And when Ralph was on the racetrack, he drove smart, for he knew that he couldn't afford to wreck his car every other week. He usually hung just off the lead for much of each race, being careful and waiting for other drivers to crash or drop out with mechanical difficulties. Then, just before the end of the race, when there were fewer cars on the course, Ralph would make his move to the lead. As one rival later recalled, "If it was a hundred-lap race, he would run second for ninety-eight laps then win the race." He didn't always win, but he won often enough to be recognized as one of the best drivers in the Sportsman division. In fact, in 1956 he won the NASCAR Sportsman championship. And more than thirty years later, he was selected as one of the top fifty drivers in NASCAR history, a rare honor for someone who raced in the Sportsman division.

Other drivers respected him, both for his ability on the track and for his behavior. Ralph wasn't a big talker, but when he spoke, he usually said something important. He was slow to anger and loyal to his friends. They nicknamed him "Ironheart."

After each race, the family would drive back home, usually arriving late at night. Then Martha would cook up a big midnight breakfast of country ham and eggs for the family and Ralph's friends, and they would discuss the race until dawn. Dale loved those times, listening to the talk about cars and racing.

If he had had a choice, chances are Dale would have done nothing but work on cars and race. As he grew older, he spent more and more time in the garage with his dad, learning how to work on cars himself, fetching tools for his father and cleaning up. Ralph knew Dale loved racing, but he also wanted his son to get an education and constantly kept on him to do better in school.

Those words went in one of Dale's ears and out the other. Although he was smart and good with his hands, during the school day he dreamed about cars and racing, once admitting, "All I ever thought about was racing." He had a go-cart and was already participating in local go-cart races, learning the basics of driving and engine repair. Apart from racing, the only other sports he ever participated in were junior high wrestling and slot car racing, the sport in which he won his first trophy.

The only time Dale and his father ever fought was over Dale's performance in school. At the time, children were allowed to quit school after eighth grade. Dale wanted to quit. His father said no.

Dale started ninth grade, quit, then after a big argument with his father, returned to school, then quit again. For a while Dale and his father, a man of few words, barely spoke.

"It was the only thing I let my daddy down over," Dale once recalled. Later in life, Dale realized that

Ralph had been right. "I should have listened to my father," he once told a reporter, further admitting that because of his lack of education, "they do things with race cars I don't understand. . . . The crew members are at the point you need an engineering degree to understand them."

But when Dale was growing up, it was different. Then, you could pick up all you needed to know about racing and cars by hanging around a garage and a racetrack. So that's what Dale did in his teenage years.

On the track and in the garage, Dale was all business. Off the track, however, he was a handful. He was full of energy. "Wild and crazy, young and dumb" was how he later described himself during those years. He stayed out late, drove too fast, and chased girls. He didn't get in any serious trouble, but he was something of a prankster. Once he convinced some friends to go over to his brother-in-law's house in the middle of the night and announce through a loudspeaker that the house was surrounded and anyone inside should come out with their hands up. His friends did so and then drove off, laughing — only to find out moments later that they were being chased by the police! Dale hadn't sent them to his brother-in-law's house, but to the home of a local police officer!

Around Kannapolis, few people who knew Dale believed he would ever settle down or amount to much. They gave Ironheart's son a nickname — "Ironhead." It was not a compliment.

As if to prove them wrong, Dale stubbornly insisted that he was old enough to make his own decisions and at age seventeen married his girlfriend. The young couple almost immediately realized the marriage was a mistake and soon divorced, but not before bearing a son, Kerry Earnhardt, in 1969.

Dale worked odd jobs for pocket money, but he really wanted to start racing. He was determined to follow in his father's footsteps to the racetrack. In 1970, his neighbors, Ray and David Oliver, gave him his first race car, an old 1956 Ford Victoria.

Ralph had long since realized how strong Dale's commitment to racing was. In fact, Dale would learn later in life that his father always believed his son would become a world-class racer. Following this belief, Ralph put aside his objections and joined his son in turning the donated car into a racer. Dale and his dad spent hours working on the car. Ralph rebuilt the engine and gave Dale some old tires. Dale and his friends fine-tuned the car and prepared it for the racetrack.

The roof of the car was painted purple and looked fine, but the rest of the body was a mess. Dale decided to paint the car and selected a shade of green that he thought would look good with the purple roof.

Dale soon discovered he wasn't much of a car painter. After mixing the paint and putting it on the car, it didn't turn out green, but pink! Out of paint, there was nothing he could do about the color, so he added simply the number "K-2" to the side and started racing his pink car in small races around his hometown.

He finished tenth in his first race in 1971 and had some success on the short dirt track courses in the area, racing in the semi-modified division, and even winning a few track championships. He was quickly earning a reputation as being a little wild, racing aggressively and staying on the track even after being in an accident.

Then one day, everything changed. Ralph was always a heavy smoker, and on September 26, 1973, while rebuilding a carburetor in his garage, he suffered a massive heart attack and died.

For Dale Earnhardt, it was time to get serious.

✸ CHAPTER FOUR ✸

1973–1978

From the Back of the Pack

After Ralph Earnhardt died, Martha told Dale that his father had been talking about giving him a chance to move up the ladder and compete in NASCAR's Sportsman division. To that end, she gave her son Ralph's two cars. Here was his chance to become the driver he had always wanted to be. As Dale said later, "It left me in a situation where I had to make it on my own."

That would prove difficult. In 1972, he had married Brenda Gee, the daughter of Robert Gee, a local body-shop owner. The young couple quickly had two children, a daughter named Kelley and a son named Ralph Dale Jr. Dale Earnhardt was not yet twenty-five years old and already had a big family.

Money was not just tight, it was almost nonexistent. Earnhardt cared only about racing. He worked as a riveter for a company that made trailers, did some welding and mechanical work on the side, but spent all his free time working on the cars and thinking about racing.

Earnhardt virtually ignored his wife and children. They were living hand to mouth, and he later said they "probably should have been on welfare." He'd often have to borrow grocery money at the end of the week and hope he could win a few dollars at the track to pay it back. Everything else went into his race cars. For use as a family car, he bought old junkers, "anything we could get for two hundred dollars." Brenda quickly tired of being an afterthought in Earnhardt's life, and they divorced.

Despite this personal setback, Dale continued to focus all his money and attention on racing. The application he filled out to compete in NASCAR's Sportsman circuit said it all. On the line that asked the applicant to list "other ambitions," he wrote, "NONE!!!"

But ambition alone wasn't enough to keep him racing. Earnhardt often had to scramble just to keep his cars on the track. He befriended area mechanics, hanging around their shops instead of working.

They'd feel so sorry for him that they'd give him spare parts.

Then in early 1975, Earnhardt hit bottom. He totaled his car in a wreck in Asheville, North Carolina, and didn't have enough money for another one. In racing terms, he was at the back of the pack, out of fuel, and rolling to a stop.

He swallowed his pride and approached his former father-in-law, Robert Gee. Gee had a race car, and within a few weeks Earnhardt talked him into letting him drive it in a race. Another man, Marshall Brooks, owned a motorcycle shop and sometimes sponsored local racers. He paid Earnhardt $75 a week to put the name of the motorcycle shop on the side of his car and occasionally bought him tires and other parts.

Meanwhile, as a sport and a business, NASCAR was just beginning to take off. A few top teams and drivers were well established, financed by sponsors and a growing pool of prize money, but many other car owners were still scrambling to put together a winning combination of car and driver. They hired and fired drivers almost week to week, hoping to find someone who could win.

In May 1975, Earnhardt got a small break. Ed Negre, a NASCAR driver and car owner, needed someone to race his #8 blue and yellow Dodge in an upcoming NASCAR event in Charlotte, North Carolina, the Charlotte 600. Dale Earnhardt was a friend of Norman Negre, Ed's son. After Norman got his friend and his father together, Negre hired Dale to drive for him.

Although Earnhardt had seen NASCAR races before, actually driving in one was a little overwhelming. There were thousands of fans and the field included drivers he had only seen at a distance before, like the legendary Richard Petty and Cale Yarborough. He knew this was his big chance and was determined not to do anything stupid that might wreck it — or the car.

It would have made a nice story if the brash young driver from nowhere exploded on the scene with an impressive performance, but that didn't happen. Racing in a big NASCAR event was a lot different from racing in the Sportsman division, and it showed in Earnhardt's driving.

Earnhardt started the race in thirty-third place. Negre's car wasn't very fast, but Dale still finished the race in twenty-second place — far behind the winner, but earning $1,925 in prize money. That wasn't good enough for Negre, however, and the race was Earnhardt's last NASCAR appearance in 1975.

From 1976 to 1977, he raced three more times in NASCAR events, but none of his appearances left much of an impression. He was improving as a driver, but in the big NASCAR races he simply didn't have a car fast enough to allow him to use his skills.

His big break came on July 4, 1978, at the Fire-Cracker 400 in Daytona. Driving a Ford for sponsor Carolina Tractor, Earnhardt came in seventh place. That surprising performance caught the eye of California businessman Rod Osterlund. Osterlund sponsored two NASCAR cars. He was dissatisfied with the performance of his driver, Dave Marcis. After Earnhardt's strong finish at the FireCracker 400, he began to ask around about the young driver.

Fortunately, Earnhardt was good friends with several mechanics who worked for Osterlund. They liked Earnhardt and encouraged Osterlund to give him a chance. He did, asking Earnhardt to drive his second car in the next-to-last race of the season.

Earnhardt sensed that this was his chance. His friends had told him that if Marcis didn't do well in the race, Earnhardt could take over as Osterlund's lead driver.

For the first time in his NASCAR career, Earnhardt displayed the hard-charging style that would soon make him one of the most popular drivers in the sport. He impressed both fans and fellow drivers with his aggressiveness and driving ability.

The only person not impressed was Dave Marcis. At one point in the race, Marcis and Earnhardt entered a corner running side by side. Marcis was the more experienced driver and expected Earnhardt to back off and let him move ahead.

Earnhardt had other ideas, and the two cars entered the turn together. Marcis decided to let Earnhardt know how he felt, and smacked Earnhardt's car door to door. He thought the move would intimidate Earnhardt.

But Dale Earnhardt was not easily intimidated. Instead of backing off, Earnhardt gave Marcis a taste of his own medicine. *Boom!* This time, he banged into Marcis.

NASCAR fans loved seeing a driver who could give it back as well as he could take it. Earnhardt continued his hard driving for the rest of the race and finished in fourth place. It wasn't a victory, but it was close.

Marcis was angry after the race. He couldn't believe that the driver of his team's number two car had treated him that way — and received applause for doing so. At the end of the season, he quit Osterlund's team.

Now Osterlund needed a new number one driver. He asked Earnhardt to take Marcis's place.

True to form, Dale Earnhardt would make the most of his opportunity. He had always believed that all he needed was a chance. Osterlund was prepared to give him one, and Earnhardt was determined to take advantage of it.

★ CHAPTER FIVE ★

1979–1980

Champion

For the first time in his racing life, Dale Earnhardt had a little money and a little security. He took part in five races in 1978 and earned over $20,000. To Earnhardt, that felt like a fortune. Now, entering the 1979 season as Osterlund's lead driver, he could drive full-time and not worry about how he was going to pay his bills. Still, it wasn't going to be easy.

At the time, NASCAR was dominated by some of the most legendary names in the history of the sport. Richard Petty was widely recognized as not only the best NASCAR driver of the time, but the best ever. His father, Lee, had been one of NASCAR's first big stars, winning the first Daytona 500 and three NASCAR season championships. Richard Petty, however, had trumped his father's legacy. Since entering his first NASCAR race in 1958, Petty had become NASCAR's most successful driver, in terms of both wins and prize money. In 1967, he won an incredible twenty-seven races, dominating the sport like no one else.

In recent years, however, he finally had some competition from stars like David Pearson, Cale Yarborough, Bobby Allison, and a few others. It seemed as if one of the same five or six drivers won every race. There was perhaps no more difficult time in the history of the sport to break through and become a big winner. The older drivers took care of one another, often teaming up to thwart a less established driver. No rookie had won a Grand National NASCAR race since 1974.

Still, while drivers like Petty and Yarborough were popular with longtime fans, some people in NASCAR were beginning to look to the future. If NASCAR was to continue to grow, the sport needed a young driver who could help lead it into a new era. No one knew who that would be — yet.

At the beginning of the 1979 season, Earnhardt,

driving Osterlund's Monte Carlo sporting #2, was optimistic thanks to his good showing at the end of the 1978 season. But it takes much more than a good driver and fast car to win a NASCAR race. It takes a great deal of teamwork, from the garage to the pits to the driver's seat. While Osterlund spent money on his cars and employed some top-notch mechanics, the pit crew wasn't the best.

Often, the pit crew is the key to a race. As soon as the car pulls into the pit, the members of the crew leap out and begin working on it. One man dumps fuel into the gas tank while another cleans the windshield. A third man jacks the car up so others can quickly remove the lug nuts from the tires, take off the old ones, and put on new ones. If they do their job well, a car can receive four brand-new tires and a full load of fuel in only thirteen or fourteen seconds. But if the crew messes up, it can take twice as long. Since every second counts in NASCAR, a fast pit stop can be the difference in a race.

The pit crew chief also has to assess the race and communicate with the driver, telling him when to pit and deciding which tires to change. Although today they use radios to stay in constant contact with the driver, when Earnhardt started racing they wrote instructions on a blackboard and held them up for the driver to read as he rocketed by. If the crew boss makes the wrong decision about tires or miscalculates the amount of fuel a driver needs, it can cost the driver the race.

In the first few races of the 1979 season, Earnhardt's car was fast enough to win, and many observers noted that Earnhardt was a skilled and entertaining driver. But the team wasn't working well together. Pit stops had been a problem. Osterlund was disappointed and replaced his crew chief with a man named Jake Elder.

Under Elder, Earnhardt's crew got its act together. Before the Volunteer 500 at the Bristol International Speedway, the entire team felt they had a chance to win.

Several days before each race, drivers have to run speed trials around the track to qualify for the race. Such trials ensure that each car can run fast enough to compete in the race safely. Qualifying also determines where each car will start. The faster a driver goes, the better his starting position. The fastest driver gets to start on the left side of the front row, in what is called the pole position.

Earnhardt qualified in the ninth spot, good but not great. Still, in the final hours before the race, Earnhardt's team continued to work on the car. By the time the race started, they were convinced they had the fastest car in the field. If Earnhardt did his job and the pit crew did theirs, the team felt there was no reason they couldn't win the race. Although the grueling 250-mile race would require five hundred laps around the half-mile track, everyone on the team was confident.

After a clean start, it wasn't long before Earnhardt noticed that he was having a few problems with the way the car was handling. As he entered and exited turns, the front end of the car felt a little "loose," making it difficult to keep the car going straight.

He came roaring in for a pit stop and explained the problem. Elder made a few quick adjustments, and although it still wasn't perfect, Earnhardt told him, "I can live with it."

Apart from that one small problem, the car was running great. Each time Earnhardt slipped behind a car in front of him — a tactic known as "drafting," which cuts down on the wind resistance on the trailing car and allows it to go faster — his car felt fast and quick. Then, when he pulled out from behind to pass and floored the accelerator, the car responded quickly with an extra surge of power that made it easy and safe to pass.

Earnhardt rapidly moved up. But after more than 130 laps, pole winner Buddy Baker still led, as he had from the start.

For the next seventy laps or so, Earnhardt, Baker, and several other drivers traded first place back and forth. Then Earnhardt got a little luck. Baker's car was bounced from the race in a crash with Cale Yarborough. That left only Earnhardt, Darrell Waltrip, and Bobby Allison in the lead pack.

The three drivers stretched out their lead and soon lapped the field. Unless there was a major accident, one of the three would win the race.

It all came down to the performance of Earnhardt's pit crew. Over the final third of the race, each time Earnhardt, Allison, and Waltrip entered the pits, Earnhardt's crew got him back on the track faster than the other two drivers. That little jump helped Earnhardt extend his lead. Waltrip was a close second until just a few laps from the finish, when Allison passed him. But Allison wasn't fast enough to catch Earnhardt. At the end of lap five hundred, Earnhardt was the one who saw the checkered flag. He had won his first NASCAR race!

Earnhardt could hardly believe it. "This is a bigger thrill than winning my first race," he blurted out soon after. "This is a win in the big leagues, against the top-caliber drivers. It wasn't some dirt track back home."

The victory was only the fourth ever by a rookie NASCAR driver and earned Earnhardt almost $20,000. Just as importantly, it qualified Osterlund's team to receive a total of almost $200,000 over the rest of the season in appearance money. That was a huge boost for the team. As Elder said afterward, "When we qualified for the race, we didn't receive tires or nothing. Now we can buy all we need." The win would enable them to buy the best equipment and compete at the highest level.

But just as important as the money was the reaction of Earnhardt's fellow drivers. If they had overlooked the rookie before, they wouldn't do so anymore. Everyone was impressed. Darrell Waltrip said, "He was the one to beat, but I couldn't do it. Dale ran a real good race."

Earnhardt made sure to thank the other drivers, many of whom had given him advice in the past. "I kind of wonder," said Earnhardt jokingly, "if they'll all hush up now."

But Jake Elder's comments proved to be the most accurate. "I really believe this is just a start," he said. "If he doesn't get hurt, he's got at least twelve good years ahead of him."

As the 1979 season went on, it was clear to everyone that it was going to be a very good year for Dale Earnhardt. He challenged for the lead in nearly every race and finished in the top ten more than half the time.

He also received a stark lesson in the dangers of racing. At the Coca-Cola 500 at the Pocono Raceway, Earnhardt was leading the race. Unlike many drivers, however, Earnhardt wasn't content just to be ahead. He kept pushing his car, trying to stretch out his lead.

No stranger to accidents on the track, Earnhardt was able to walk away from this crash in 1982 despite an injured leg.

Earnhardt waves to the cheering crowd after winning the Busch
Classic in February 1986.

Earnhardt mulls over an upcoming race in late 1986.

Earnhardt's signature sunglasses reflect the checkered flag.

AP/Wide World Photos

Earnhardt streaks across the finish line in first place at the Brickyard 400 in August of 1995.

It's easy to see why one of Earnhardt's nicknames is the Intimidator!

Earnhardt runs neck and neck with Ken Schrader during a lap of the 2001 Daytona 500.

Dale Sr. and Dale Jr. celebrate the elder's victory at IROC in 2000. Dale Jr. took fifth place.

This time, he pushed a little too hard. As he rocketed down the track, his car started to slide out of control until — *bam!* — it slammed against the wall. Inside the car, Earnhardt took a big hit, too, despite his seat belt and shoulder harness. As debris from the car flew through the air, pain shot through his upper body.

When rescuers reached Earnhardt, he was in agony. He was transported to the hospital and doctors determined that he had broken both collarbones. As Earnhardt said later, "The doctor in charge told me that judging from the way my collarbones were broken, it was an act of God my neck wasn't broken, too."

Collarbone fractures can take a long time to heal. They are particularly bothersome to race car drivers, who use their arms, shoulders, and upper body to steer the car and shift gears. It appeared as if Earnhardt's season was over.

Earnhardt had other ideas. Four weeks later, he was back on the track. He was still in pain, but he could drive the car.

Although Earnhardt didn't win another race in

1979, he was named Rookie of the Year. He finished seventh in NASCAR's points championship and earned close to $250,000. In one short year, he had become one of NASCAR's best drivers.

Earnhardt couldn't help but attract interest from sponsors who were trying to change the image of NASCAR. Most people thought of the sport as a bunch of country boys driving hot rods. Major sponsors wanted drivers who projected a more sophisticated image, were comfortable around businessmen, and could therefore help sell the sport.

Earnhardt, despite his youth, looked and acted like an old-time NASCAR driver. He had unruly hair, and a massive mustache dominated his face. His voice sounded like he'd just stepped out of the backwoods. Critics who looked at and listened to him didn't think he had what it took to represent the sport. Although they respected his driving ability, few thought that he would ever become the "face of NASCAR."

They were wrong. Earnhardt appealed to the sport's most die-hard fans, the regular people who worked hard all week and wanted to have some fun on the weekend. They liked the way he raced and didn't care how he talked or looked. He was one of them. As one observer noted, "People subconsciously become the driver of that car. [Earnhardt's] a kid who came from the bottom, worked hard for everything he got, and didn't have any airs about him — that's what we say in the South when people get snooty. Truck drivers, dockworkers, welders, and shrimp-boat captains loved that. He was everything they dreamed about being."

In 1980, it didn't matter whether sponsors liked him or not. He got off to a quick start, finishing in the top five in each of the first four races. Then, at the Atlanta 500, he broke through to the top.

His win in 1979 had come at a "short-track" less than a mile in circumference. NASCAR's big races — and the big money — were those events held at "super speedways," longer tracks with long straightaways that enabled the drivers to race at much higher speeds. Earnhardt had yet to win on such a super speedway. If he were ever to be recognized as the best, that's what he would have to do.

The Atlanta 500 was just such a race. During qualifying, however, things didn't look good. His car had engine trouble and he qualified a full second slower than pole winner Buddy Baker. His starting position was way back in the pack, and few observers gave him much of a chance to win.

The first part of the race was marred by a number of small accidents and caution flags. Cale Yarborough took command as Earnhardt slowly moved up.

On lap 169, Donnie Allison (Bobby Allison's brother) took the lead, with Yarborough right behind him. Earnhardt and Terry Labonte then managed to catch the leaders, and the four cars raced around the track in a big knot, Yarborough and Earnhardt on the inside, Allison and Labonte on the outside. Then, on lap 202, Allison and Labonte got tangled up and hit the wall. Both drivers fell out of contention as others moved into the lead pack under the yellow flag.

With just under fifty laps left, Yarborough and Earnhardt worked together to gain ground on new leader Bobby Allison. Each man drafted behind the other to save fuel while maintaining top speed.

Suddenly, on lap 300, Yarborough's engine failed. Earnhardt continued to charge and then blew past Allison. After that, no one would catch him. As he said later, he just kept praying, "Don't let me have a flat tire."

The victory in Atlanta put Earnhardt into first place in the points race. It also made him a target of the other drivers. Suddenly veteran drivers who'd helped out Ralph Earnhardt's boy weren't so helpful anymore. In fact, they seemed determined to knock him out of first place.

That didn't slow Earnhardt down. Two weeks later, he won his second straight 500 at Bristol, and then placed in the top ten seven times in his next eleven races! Then, in mid-July, Earnhardt was leading the Nashville 420 when Cale Yarborough came up on him from behind. The duel between the two men over the final laps had the crowd on its feet.

Time and time again, Yarborough came up on Earnhardt, only to be cut off. On several occasions, he bumped the leader with his car, hoping to make Earnhardt back off.

It didn't work. Earnhardt powered to another win.

He won two more races for the season, giving him a total of five for the year. He was the points champion once again, making him the first driver ever to be named rookie of the year and points champ in back-to-back seasons.

Whether NASCAR liked it or not, the face of NASCAR was becoming Dale Earnhardt, standing in front of his battered car, sporting a big grin, and holding a trophy over his head.

★ CHAPTER SIX ★

1981–1983

Checkered Flags

Now that Dale Earnhardt had reached the top, he wanted to stay there. He would soon learn that would be difficult.

Earnhardt liked his team and his crew. After his first year with Osterlund, he had signed a five-year contract with the owner.

But the team didn't get off to a good start in 1981. Osterlund was thinking about getting out of racing, and his waning interest in the sport showed in the team's performance on the track. Neither Earnhardt's car nor his pit crew was top-notch. Dale was still driving as well as ever, but instead of finishing in first place, he was finishing farther back. He was competitive but just couldn't win.

Halfway through the 1981 season, Osterlund

decided to get out of racing altogether. He sold his team to another man, Jim Stacy.

Stacy made some changes to the team, few of which Earnhardt supported. After only four races, Earnhardt was allowed to break his contract and leave.

Luckily, he had a place to go. His friend, former driver Richie Childress, had just started his own team. The two men respected each other, and Earnhardt raced for Childress for the remainder of the season.

But starting a new race team is hard. It costs a great deal of money, and the team owner and his drivers have to court sponsors for money. They also have to hire the pit crew and mechanics. Since most of the best men are already with established teams, they often have to start from scratch, taking a chance on younger men and hoping they develop.

The team worked hard, but by the end of the season Earnhardt had failed to win a race. After coming in first the year before, he finished in seventh place in the points championship.

After the season, Childress and Earnhardt took stock of the situation. Childress knew that the inexperienced and underfunded team was hurting Earnhardt's chances to win. Meanwhile, a bigger, more established car owner named Bud Moore was after Earnhardt.

Childress told Earnhardt he should accept the offer, telling him he was "too good a driver for my team." Although he regretted leaving his friend, Earnhardt agreed and reluctantly joined Moore's team.

But that wasn't the only change in Earnhardt's life. Now that he had attained some success, he was able to do what he hadn't before, namely, be a provider to his children. Dale Jr. and Kerry had lived with their father since 1980. Earnhardt was able to pay for their education and give them things they had never had before. Regrettably, however, he wasn't able to spend much time with them. Racing was consuming his life.

He was famous now, and people were beginning to treat him differently. Even though he had moved from Kannapolis to nearby Mooresville, he had always been able to hang out with his old friends, playing horseshoes and just relaxing. Now, however, people he barely knew were showing up unexpectedly, and he began to slowly withdraw from many of his old friends.

Earnhardt needed someone he could depend on to stand by him. Nearly ten years earlier, when he was still racing in the Sportsman division, he had met a young teenage girl named Teresa, the daughter of a friend he met through racing. Several years later, when Teresa was a young woman, they began dating, and after the 1982 season, they married. After being in two marriages that failed in part because of all the time he spent racing, Earnhardt was determined not to let that happen again. Teresa became a part of the team. She helped take care of the boys and took on an important role in managing his career.

Earnhardt got off to a slow start with Bud Moore's team at the start of the 1982 season. He ran well but just couldn't seem to win, or even finish, a race. Several times he was forced to quit due to mechanical problems. It was beginning to look like the former champion and rookie of the year was turning out to be a bust.

Entering the Rebel 500 at the Darlington International Raceway, Earnhardt had gone thirty-nine races without a victory. He started the race in fifth place and narrowly avoided several wrecks. Then, as the field thinned out, he took command. The end of the race came down to a battle between Earnhardt and Cale Yarborough.

Going into the last lap, Earnhardt's #15 Thunderbird held a narrow lead over his veteran rival. As Earnhardt made his way around the track, Yarborough hung on his back bumper, inches away. He knew that Earnhardt had the faster car. He figured he had only one chance to win, passing Earnhardt coming out of the final turn. If he edged ahead, Earnhardt wouldn't have time to make a move to take back the lead.

As the two cars roared out of the corner, Yarborough made his move. Coming out of the turn, he steered his car down low and tried to slingshot past Earnhardt on the inside.

Earnhardt anticipated the move. He, too, moved a little to the inside. He didn't cut off Yarborough completely, but he forced him farther down the track than he liked, cutting the slingshot short. Both men then floored the accelerator and gunned toward the checkered flag. The crowd roared as two of NASCAR's best drivers went flat out to the finish line.

For a split second, the two cars were almost even, and then Earnhardt inched ahead. As Earnhardt said after the race in his own typically understated style, "I couldn't see Cale out of my left window, so I figured I had finished ahead."

He had, winning by half a car length. Earnhardt was back in the winner's circle.

Still, the victory would prove to be his only win of the 1982 season. In fact, his overall performance was even worse than it had been in 1981. He finished twelfth in the points championship.

Earnhardt was beginning to get frustrated, and when he became frustrated, he drove even harder and took even more chances than he normally did. Late in the 1982 season, Earnhardt's competition began complaining that Earnhardt was reckless, and NASCAR fined him for his overly aggressive driving.

But that didn't stop Earnhardt. If anything, it made him even more determined, because he knew he wasn't aggressive to be nasty but to win races.

In the 125-mile qualifying race for Daytona, he proved that he could run smart, too. For much of the race, he ran just behind Indy Car legend A. J. Foyt, saying later, "I was just where I wanted to be." Veteran Buddy Baker hung on Earnhardt's bumper.

Then, on the final lap, Earnhardt saw Baker start to swing low to pass both men. Quick as a wink, Earnhardt swung down, too, knowing that Baker, running so closely behind him, would inadvertently give Earnhardt's car a subtle aerodynamic "push." Earnhardt took advantage and swept past Foyt to win the race.

It was a brilliant, classic move, one that Earnhardt hoped would spark him to a win in the Daytona 500. But racing's biggest prize continued to elude him.

The rest of 1982 and 1983 followed a familiar pattern, the occasional spectacular win followed by long droughts. Earnhardt battled car problems and some bad luck and won only two more races. Half the time he didn't even finish in the top ten.

Meanwhile, Richie Childress has been slowly building his team. In 1983, with driver Ricky Rudd, they began to enjoy some success.

Childress and Earnhardt had remained friends. Earnhardt, his wife, and their infant daughter Taylor moved to a big house on three hundred acres, which included a ten-acre lake. During the winter, the two men went hunting and fishing together. While they were out in the woods, they rehashed the previous season.

Childress thought his team had made a lot of progress. Earnhardt agreed, so when Childress asked him if he wanted to rejoin the team, Earnhardt jumped at the chance.

⋆ CHAPTER SEVEN ⋆

1984–1997

The Intimidator

Dale Earnhardt's return to driving for Richie Childress would prove to be the key moment in his NASCAR career. Over the next decade, despite significant changes in the sport, he would enjoy more success than any other driver. He became more than just a winning driver. He became a legend.

Earnhardt took the track in 1984 in a new car, a Chevy Monte Carlo, and a new number, #3. For the rest of his career, Earnhardt and the #3 car would be the most feared combination in NASCAR.

It didn't happen overnight, though. It took Earnhardt and the Childress team a while to get their engines revving just right. Over the first part of the year, Earnhardt and the Childress team got to know each other, testing equipment and learning how to get the most out of both the car and the driver.

Then, at the Talladega 500 in July 1984, it all came together.

The Alabama track is an incredibly fast 2.55-mile tri-oval, and cars regularly reached speeds in excess of 200 miles per hour. Earnhardt had won Talladega the previous year and in 1984 was part of the ten-car lead pack going into the final lap. Terry Labonte led the race, with Earnhardt and Buddy Baker drafting close behind. Labonte expected Earnhardt to try a slingshot pass coming out of one of the turns, using the draft to swing inside and take the lead.

In turn one in the final lap, Labonte cut Earnhardt off, swinging low. Earnhardt remained patient. Heading into the second turn, Labonte slowed slightly, again thwarting Earnhardt's plans. And in turn three, Labonte again ran low.

This time, Earnhardt was ready. As the cars swung out of the turn, Earnhardt went high on Labonte's right side.

It was a risky move, for by taking the outside track Earnhardt had to cover more ground than the leader. He was also concerned that Baker might swing down low and try to slingshot past Labonte himself.

But Earnhardt got lucky. Baker followed his lead and gave Earnhardt a small push. It was just enough to send his car past Labonte. As they left the turn, Earnhardt pulled into the lead, his engine roaring. He hung on to capture his first victory in thirty races.

"I guess," he said after his first winning race with his new team, "I've proven I can win in any car." Labonte put it even more simply. "Dale just ran me down," he said.

Unfortunately, for the rest of the season Earnhardt would win just one more race and fell behind in the points championship, finishing fourth. It was a good start for the Childress team, but there was still room for improvement.

In 1985, Earnhardt's performance in a series of races really got the public's attention. His background racing on dirt tracks made him a bit more comfortable racing in the short-track races than on the super speedways. While the pace is slower on a short track, the tracks are narrower, too. Drivers have to race in a single line and then make daring passes just like on the old dirt tracks. NASCAR's younger drivers had very little experience in such racing, giving Earnhardt a big advantage.

He raced hard and tough on the short tracks, winning four such races in 1985. He also made a few enemies. Earnhardt wasn't afraid of making contact with other cars on the track, and after most of these races his car sported more than a few dents and scrapes of paint. Fans loved seeing such hard racing, but one losing driver complained and said, "They can't allow him to continue to do it."

Earnhardt's aggressive style made him the man to watch out for. Wherever he raced, he was in the back of every driver's mind. All race long they looked in the rearview mirror and worried what he might do. Sometimes they'd back off instead of challenging him. This gave Earnhardt a tremendous advantage and earned him the nickname that would stick with him for the remainder of his career: "The Intimidator."

Despite the four wins, Earnhardt slipped down to eighth place in the points standings. He and Childress knew they would have to improve their performance if they were ever to win another points title.

Fortunately, two strong seasons gave them plenty of resources to build a better team. Both men realized that races were won in the garage almost as much as on the track. They kept expanding their operation, buying more high-tech equipment and doing everything possible to ensure they were putting the best car they could on the track. Then it was up to Earnhardt.

In 1986, the Intimidator began to earn yet another nickname: "The Dominator." From the first race, it was clear that Earnhardt had one of the top cars in NASCAR. At the TranSouth 500 at Darlington, South Carolina, he picked up his first win, taking the lead on lap five and staying there an incredible 335 laps out of 367. At one point he even led the race by 22.5 seconds and had lapped all but one car in the field. That just doesn't happen in a NASCAR race. Fans went crazy.

He showed his versatility in the longest race of the season, the Coca-Cola 600 at the Charlotte Motor Speedway. Earnhardt, who once recalled "standing on a flatbed truck watching this race with my daddy," considered the 1.5-mile egg-shaped track his home turf and in 1986 ran one of the cleanest races of his career, driving strategically before zooming in front.

The win temporarily silenced some of his critics.

Earlier in the year, Earnhardt had been fined by NASCAR for bumping another car and causing an accident. He gave no one anything to complain about in Charlotte, apart from their place in the standings. The victory gave him a big lead in the points championship, and he won the title going away that year, his first since 1980.

Now that Earnhardt was on top, he wanted to stay there. As he later said, "I wasn't mature enough when I won the first title. I respect it and enjoy it more now that I know what is at stake."

In 1987, he responded with the greatest season of his career. It was also his most controversial.

From the very start, Earnhardt dominated the season on and off the track. He won six of the first eight races, taking a big lead in the points standings and earning the Childress team a new lucrative sponsorship deal with General Motors worth more than a million dollars a year. At the same time, more and more drivers began to complain about Earnhardt's style on the track. They were simply tired of being intimidated by the Intimidator.

Earnhardt made no apologies, either for his performance or his style. But those who cared to could find reasons for the clashes. Earnhardt had always driven hard, but NASCAR was changing. When Earnhardt first started racing, every driver drove to win in every race. If he didn't, he wouldn't be driving very long.

But now so much money was coming into NASCAR that some drivers played it safe. They didn't try to win, they just tried to stay out of trouble and finish the race, for that was enough to earn a fine salary. Their cautious style and Earnhardt's aggressive approach made conflict almost inevitable.

At the same time, the cars were becoming much faster and more powerful. At higher speeds, the bumps and nudges that had been a part of NASCAR racing for years became even more dangerous. And as the older drivers who had been brought up like Earnhardt left NASCAR, fewer of the new drivers knew how to react to such tactics. When they tried, they often crashed. They just didn't have Dale Earnhardt's combination of experience and talent.

Unlike these younger drivers, Earnhardt expected to be bumped, so when it happened he didn't go running to race officials or the media to air his complaints. He did his talking on the track, with his race car.

NASCAR had to treat the situation with care. They wanted to appease the younger drivers, but at the same time they realized that Earnhardt was making the sport more popular and that was helping everyone, even his critics, earn more money than ever before.

Earnhardt wrapped up the points championship before the season was over, the first driver in NASCAR history to do so. He was at the top of his sport, but that didn't mean he was standing still.

Earnhardt had always driven a yellow and blue car. In 1987, his team decided to change colors, to go for something more distinctive that reflected Earnhardt's personal and racing style.

For inspiration, they looked at other successful sports franchises. The Oakland Raiders of the National Football League had a rough-and-ready, rebellious outlaw image. Earnhardt fans considered him cut from the same cloth — an outsider, a guy who made his own rules and dared the competition to challenge him. Earnhardt's team adopted the same silver and black color combination used by the Raiders.

It was a big hit. Earnhardt-related memorabilia like T-shirts, hats, and other items had always been popular, but few fans wore combinations of yellow and blue away from the racetrack. Silver and black, however, went with everything. Earnhardt items instantly became big sellers, and fans started calling him "the Man in Black."

There was another big change in NASCAR, one that would alter the sport forever.

During the race at Talladega in 1987, Bill Elliott had set a record by qualifying at the super speedway with a lap of almost 213 miles per hour — the fastest lap ever run in the history of NASCAR. Everyone was running faster and faster.

Later, during the race itself, Bobby Allison was jetting down the front stretch when he blew a tire and his car started sliding. He was going so fast that his car became airborne right in front of the stands. It sailed over the concrete wall into the protective fence in front of the flag stand.

Fortunately, although a section of the fence was destroyed, the fence held and Allison wasn't badly hurt. The race was delayed for several hours while the fence was repaired. But NASCAR officials realized they had been extremely lucky. Had the fence not held up, Allison's car would have ended up in the grandstand. Dozens, perhaps hundreds of fans could have been hurt or killed. NASCAR decided they had to do something to slow down the cars.

In the 1988 season, they required cars running at the fastest tracks to use what were known as restrictor plates, a small aluminum plate that limited the amount of air allowed into the engine, cutting horsepower and slowing the cars down. In effect, that set an upper limit on how fast the cars could be driven and made every car run at more or less the same top speed.

Although at first the plates were required at only a few tracks, since then they have been required at more and more racetracks. They have dramatically affected racing. Before plates, the field often stretched over a number of laps. Drivers stayed in small packs as they moved up and back in the field.

Now it is possible for most drivers to stay close and run in one or two big packs. While it has slowed the cars down and kept them from becoming airborne, cars are so closely packed that the number of multi-car accidents that knock out a lot of drivers at once have skyrocketed.

Old-time drivers like Earnhardt disliked the restriction. He felt it was less safe and made driving more complicated. Instead of using the car's power to pass, drivers have to learn to use the air, drafting off one another and trying to stay out of turbulence. That causes cars to stay bunched together, and with less room to maneuver on the track, it becomes harder to pass and avoid trouble.

Despite the changes, Earnhardt continued to dominate, but after a few early wins in 1988, he was dogged by mechanical difficulties. Still, even though he ended the season with only three victories, he finished in the top ten in two-thirds of the races to finish third in the points standings.

He finished second in 1989 before regaining the title in 1990 with nine first-place finishes, earning more than 1.3 million dollars, a NASCAR record. He followed with yet another title in 1991. Although he knew it would be impossible to match Richard Petty's record of two hundred victories, with five point titles under his belt, Earnhardt looked ahead to having the opportunity to match Petty's NASCAR record of seven point championships.

But success also brought problems. In 1992, the team's longtime crew chief, Kirk Shelmerdine, announced he was leaving after the season. Although Earnhardt hoped to send him out on a high note, he had his worst season in more than a decade, winning only once and finishing twelfth in the points title.

Some observers blamed Shelmerdine, but others thought Earnhardt was at fault. He was now worth millions of dollars and had formed his own company to handle his investments, Dale Earnhardt Incorporated, or DEI. In addition, Earnhardt raised chickens and Black Angus cattle, was beginning to put together his own race team for his sons, and manufactured souvenirs and clothing. Although he hired others to run the day-to-day operation and Teresa was heavily involved, it was still a lot of responsibility.

There were also a lot of benefits. He knew that he was providing for his family, not just in the present but for the future. His wealth also enabled him to give to charities and support other causes. Once, after a big storm ruined the corn crop near his North

Carolina headquarters, he bought new seed corn for all the farmers.

Still, after his dismal 1992 season, people were starting to whisper that Earnhardt's days as the Dominator were over. He was determined to prove them wrong.

★ CHAPTER EIGHT ★

1993–1998

Daytona and Other Dreams

Dale Earnhardt was now entering his fifteenth year in NASCAR. He had attained great fame and fortune, but he still had several goals. He wanted to match or surpass Richard Petty's record. He wanted to see his sons, Dale and Kerry, succeed in racing, and he wanted to win the Daytona 500, the biggest race in NASCAR. Some people were beginning to say he was cursed and would never be able to win that race. He knew that until he did, some people would say his career was incomplete.

In 1993, he made great strides to reaching goal number one, as he bounced back to capture another points title. It came at an important time for NASCAR, as the season was marred by the death of 1992 champion Alan Kulwicki in a plane crash and the loss of veteran Donnie Allison in a helicopter accident.

Earnhardt provided the only bright spot in an otherwise tragic season. In May, at the Coca-Cola 600 in Charlotte, he drove one of the most remarkable races of his career.

By NASCAR standards, the first half of the race was boring. Earnhardt seemed to sense that, and in the middle of the race he made things exciting.

Leading the race, he came in for a pit stop going way too fast. Race officials slapped him with a fifteen-second penalty, apparently knocking him from the race. But Earnhardt managed to pick his way through the field, getting back on the lead lap after a restart following an accident, then pulling into second place, half a lap behind leader Dale Jarrett.

In order to catch Jarrett, Earnhardt knew he needed a caution flag to allow him to gain ground. Coming off turn four, Earnhardt sped in behind driver Greg Sacks. All of a sudden Sacks's car started spinning. Earnhardt avoided him, and when the yellow flag came out, he pulled in behind Jarrett. But he wasn't allowed to stay there. Officials ruled that

Earnhardt had nudged Sacks on purpose, causing the spin. Sacks later said he hadn't, but Earnhardt offered only a partial denial. Nevertheless, he once again was a lap off the lead.

It didn't take him long to recover. He managed to get back on the lead lap, then, after another yellow flag, he reached the lead pack. From there, he never looked back — he kept on moving up to win the race going away. It was one of the most memorable victories of his career.

He carried the momentum from 1993 into 1994. Although he won only four times, he was competitive in virtually every race, finishing in the top five in nearly two-thirds of the races. If he grabbed a victory in the AC Delco 500 in Rockingham, North Carolina, in October, he could wrap up his seventh title and tie Petty's mark.

He entered the 492-lap race needing only fifty points to clinch the title. But he qualified in only twentieth place and trailed for the first third of the race before taking the lead on lap 173. He dropped back, but then roared ahead to take over for good seventy-seven laps from the finish.

But victory would not come easy. Rick Mast hung

on his bumper for the final laps of the race. But as Mast said later of Earnhardt, "His bumper gets mighty wide there at the end." Each time Mast tried to pass, Earnhardt deftly cut him off.

Mast tried one last time on the last turn of the last lap, hoping to slingshot past Earnhardt on the inside. But the Dominator held on to beat him by a car length.

Earnhardt was happy and relieved after the race. "It's great to be number one," he said. "I drive a race car one hundred percent, and that's what I'll do 'til I retire." No one doubted him.

Earnhardt wasn't slowing down, on the track or off. Since Dale Junior and Kerry had moved in with him, Earnhardt had slowly grown closer to his sons, as well as to his daughter Kelley. They had had a difficult time growing up without their father.

In 1991, Kerry and Dale had expressed some interest in racing. They started working on an old 1978 Monte Carlo, fixing it up for racing.

At first their father didn't pay much attention. Like his father Ralph before him, he wasn't sure if the boys were serious.

But night after night they were out in the garage,

getting their hands dirty. Earnhardt finally stepped in and gave them a hand, putting on a roll bar and other safety equipment.

That year the brothers began racing on short tracks in the area, one brother driving one week, the other the next. Their father was impressed and offered to buy the boys identical cars for the upcoming season. Then sister Kelley spoke up. She wanted to race, too. Although female drivers were a rarity, her father bought a third car.

For the next few years, there was usually at least one Earnhardt in every short-track race in North Carolina. Although they all did well, Dale Junior seemed to have the most promise.

His father was surprised, for his youngest son had been timid growing up, unlike Kerry, who was aggressive like his father.

Once he got on the track, however, Kerry was sometimes too aggressive. Dale Jr., on the other hand, seemed to have the instinct needed to succeed as a driver. Although Kelley eventually stopped racing altogether, and Kerry, after getting married, took racing less seriously, Dale Jr. stuck with it. By the mid-1990s, he was enjoying some success in the

Busch Series, NASCAR-sponsored races that took the place of the old Sportsman division in 1982, giving younger drivers a chance to gain experience. Earnhardt was reminded of the time he and his father had raced together, and looked ahead to the day when he and Dale Jr. might one day be in the same race.

The only goal left for Earnhardt was the Daytona 500. He'd been knocking on the door for years, but somehow had never managed to win the sport's signature race. He had finished second and third a number of times and on two occasions had actually led on the last lap before falling short, once running out of fuel and another time falling back to fifth after cutting a tire on some debris.

In 1996, however, his career almost ended before he reached his goal. In the DieHard 500 at Talladega, Ernie Irvan smacked into Sterling Marlin. In a chain reaction, Marlin's car then struck Earnhardt from behind.

Earnhardt's car turned sideways, slammed into the wall, spun around, and then was hit by another vehicle. Upon impact, Earnhardt's #3 went airborne and was then struck by two more cars. Despite a broken sternum, a broken collarbone, and a badly bruised pelvis, Earnhardt managed to walk from the car.

A year later, he experienced another scary moment. In the middle of a race, he briefly lost consciousness, yet somehow managed to maintain control of his car. Doctors were unable to identify the problem and Earnhardt was allowed to keep racing, but it was a cause of concern.

By 1998, he was the sentimental favorite at Daytona, but some NASCAR fans felt that his time had come and gone. In 1995, 1996, and 1997, he had finished second, fourth, and fifth in the points race as a new generation of drivers, paced by Jeff Gordon, seemed poised to take over NASCAR. Earnhardt hadn't even won a race in 1997.

He was getting older, and some observers wondered if he still had the stamina needed to win a five-hundred-mile race, particularly one as demanding as Daytona.

The 1998 race was the signature event of NASCAR's fiftieth anniversary season and was heavily promoted. The fans weren't disappointed.

Earnhardt and other drivers traded the lead back

and forth several times before Earnhardt took the front position sixty-one laps from the finish. Near the end of the race, there was a caution flag. Earnhardt led a charge into the pits and then took a gamble.

All the drivers in the lead pack, which included Rusty Wallace and 1997 champion Jeff Gordon, needed fuel. The others opted for two new tires as well. The change took about eight seconds.

Earnhardt, however, was pleased with his tires and took a chance they'd hold up. He only took on fuel and roared out of the pits with a two-second lead. If it worked, he was a genius. If it didn't, he'd fail again.

The final laps showed NASCAR racing at its best as the drivers jockeyed for position. Gordon tried to surge ahead several times, and then fell back with some minor mechanical trouble.

On the last lap, Earnhardt, Terry Labonte, and Jeremy Mayfield were all in position to win. Earnhardt, however, would not be denied.

With a small lead, he took aim on a slower car ahead. He passed the car and was able to use it to cause Labonte and Mayfield to slow down slightly as they passed by. He let the throttle out and powered toward the finish line.

As he crossed the line, he saw what he had been hoping to see for twenty years — the checkered flag. He had won Daytona!

After his victory lap, he steered his car onto the grass and did doughnuts like some high school kid. His fans roared with laughter. That's just what they liked about Earnhardt. He always acted just as they would have.

When he walked down the pit road, all the other crew teams stood in single file and shook his hand. They knew how much the race meant to him.

In the winner's circle, he was ecstatic. "Yes! Yes!" he screamed over and over, adding, "Can you believe it?"

Then, with a sly grin, he pulled a small stuffed monkey out and waved it overhead. "The monkey's off my back!" he announced to more laughter. When NASCAR officials tried to stop some fans from pulling up the sod he'd driven over in the field, he stopped them. "Let them have it!" he said. "I'll pay for it."

Later, he admitted that it was the most emotional win of his career. "I don't think I really cried," he said, "but my eyes watered up when I saw the checkered flag."

NASCAR's Man in Black had a soft spot after all.

⋆ CHAPTER NINE ⋆

1999–2002

Finish Line Legacy

The next three years were probably the happiest of Dale Earnhardt's life. He had accomplished just about everything there was to accomplish in NASCAR. Although he wasn't the best driver on the track anymore, and the hard racing that had marked his career to that point was a thing of the past, he was still a force to be reckoned with.

Then, at Bristol in 1999, he turned back the clock. On the last lap of the race, he blew by — and through — Terry Labonte, roughly knocking his car aside and sweeping to the finish. Labonte fans were angry after the race, while Earnhardt fans nodded their heads knowingly. This was the racer they had loved for more than twenty years. NASCAR officials huddled for a long time before deciding to let Earnhardt's victory stand.

But those moments were now few and far between. Most of the time Earnhardt raced with a degree of caution he rarely expressed in years past. He was nearing the age of fifty and knew that no one above the age of forty-five had ever won the points championship. He was beginning to recognize that it would soon be time to retire and leave NASCAR to the next generation.

NASCAR had become a young person's game. Jeff Gordon had taken over as NASCAR's best-known driver and was highly skilled, but he was everything Earnhardt was not — polished, educated, and made to order for NASCAR's new generation of fans.

Many of those fans rooted for Earnhardt — but not Dale Sr. Dale Jr., who in 2000 began driving a car sponsored by DEI, quickly became one of the most popular and successful young drivers in NASCAR. Although he shared some traits with his father, Dale Jr. was also part of the new generation. His father was puzzled by his infatuation with computers and other technology. Dale Jr. didn't care for country and western music, preferring punk rock and rap. That made him popular with younger fans.

Although they had their differences, on the track,

they were equals. Earnhardt loved the notion of racing with his son. At times, when he couldn't win himself, he ran interference for Dale Jr. The rest of the time, he treated him like any other driver, trying his best to defeat him, even giving his car a gentle nudge now and then.

Before the season began, Earnhardt had neck surgery and felt better than he had since the accident at Talladega. Perhaps due to the presence of his son on the track, in 2000 Earnhardt responded with his best season since 1995.

In March, he announced that he would still be a force in the race for the points title. At the Cracker Barrel 500, he collected a big win, edging out Bobby Labonte in a photo finish by all of two inches for the closest victory of his career.

What would prove to be the final victory of his career came in October at Talladega in the Winston 500, a restrictor-plate race.

Earnhardt had always hated the restrictor plate and had often complained that he wasn't any good at racing with it. The competition knew better, and one last time Earnhardt proved that it didn't matter what kind of circumstances he was racing in, he was just very good, period.

With ten laps to go, he was in twenty-second place. No one, absolutely no one, gave him a chance to win.

Even Earnhardt wasn't quite sure how he did it. To observers, he picked his way past the other cars with a series of deft moves and knowledge of drafting that seemed well beyond anyone else on the track.

He also had a little luck. Kenny Wallace and Joe Nemechek needed some help over the final laps, too, so they teamed up with Earnhardt to draft their way toward the front. Wallace kept "bump drafting" Earnhardt, pushing him forward with his car and then drafting behind him. Then, at the end of the race, Earnhardt got a little help from Dale Jr., who managed to cause leader Mike Skinner to back off for an instant, allowing his dad to blow past for the win.

Earnhardt ended up finishing second in the race for the points title but left little doubt that the Man in Black was still the equal of anyone sitting in the driver's seat of a NASCAR car.

People started asking him if he thought he had a chance to win the title in 2001 and surpass Richard Petty's record. With a twinkle in his eye, Earnhardt would only smile. His contract with Childress ran through the 2003 season, and he laughed off talk of retirement before then. "If I can't beat the next guy or win a race, I'll stop," he said. "My reflexes and health will tell me when."

Unfortunately, the 2001 Daytona 500 ended Earnhardt's career at a time when he could still beat the next guy and win the race. Almost from the moment of his death, everyone began to realize just how much he had meant to the sport.

Never before had the death of a NASCAR driver caused such an outpouring of emotion from fans. Observers compared the reaction to those of the public after the deaths of President John F. Kennedy, Elvis Presley, and Princess Diana. All over the country, Earnhardt fans made impromptu memorials. The entrances of Daytona, DEI, and virtually every racetrack in the country were buried in flowers as fans gathered to reflect on his life and career. People painted #3's on their cars and hung black ribbons from their rearview mirrors. An invitation-only memorial service drew 3,000 people. As Dale Jr. said, "I'm sure he'd want us to go on, so that's what we're going to do."

An era of NASCAR history had ended.

A year later, however, fans got to remember Earnhardt one last time. At the 2002 Daytona 500, Dale Earnhardt Jr. honored his father in the best way possible. He went on and won the race.

Afterward, he did doughnuts in the infield, just like his dad.

Dale Earnhardt Sr.'s Career Statistics

Year	Races Entered	Wins	Top 5	Top 10	Poles	Earnings	Points Rank
1975	1 of 30	0	0	0	0	2,425 1,925	n/a
1976	2 of 30	0	0	0	0	3,085	103 104
1977	1 of 30	0	0	0	0	1,375	118
1978	5 of 30	0	1	2	0	20,745 20,145	43 44
1979	27 of 31	1	11	17	4	274,810 237,575	7
1980	31 of 31	5	19	24	0	671,990 451,360	1
1981	31 of 31	0	9	17	0	353,971 324,290	7
1982	30 of 30	1	7	12	1	400,880 357,270	12
1983	30 of 30	2	9	14	0	465,203 396,991	8
1984	30 of 30	2	12	22	0	634,670 509,805	4
1985	28 of 28	4	10	16	1	546,595 451,658	8

Year	Races Entered	Wins	Top 5	Top 10	Poles	Earnings	Points Rank
1986	29 of 29	5	16	23	1	1,768,880 868,100	1
1987	29 of 29	11	21	24	1	2,069,243 1,041,120	1
1988	29 of 29	3	13	19	0	1,214,089 739,175	3
1989	29 of 29	5	14	19	0	1,432,230 885,050	2
1990	29 of 29	9	18	23	4	3,308,056 1,307,830	1
1991	29 of 29	4	14	21	0	2,416,685 1,029,060	1
1992	29 of 29	1	6	15	1	915,463 838,385	12
1993	30 of 30	6	17	21	2	3,353,789 1,326,240	1
1994	31 of 31	4	20	25	2	3,300,733 1,465,890	1
1995	31 of 31	5	19	23	3	3,154,241 2,295,300	2
1996	31 of 31	2	13	17	2	2,285,926	4

Year	Races Entered	Wins	Top 5	Top 10	Poles	Earnings	Points Rank
1997	32 of 32	0	7	16	0	2,151,909 1,663,019	5
1998	33 of 33	1	5	13	0	2,990,749 2,611,100	8
1999	34 of 34	3	7	21	0	3,048,236 2,712,089	7
2000	34 of 34	2	13	24	0	4,918,886 3,701,390	2
2001	1 of 36	0	0	0	0	296,833	57
Totals	676	76	281	428	22	42,001,697 27,827,986	

Career Highlights

- Rookie of the Year, 1979
- Seven-time NASCAR Winston Cup Series Champion — 1980, 1986, 1987, 1990, 1991, 1993, 1994
- Five-time NMPA Driver of the Year — 1980, 1986, 1987, 1990, 1994
- Only six-time winner of the Busch Clash — 1980, 1986, 1988, 1991, 1993, 1995
- Only three-time winner of the Winston All-Star Race — 1987, 1990, 1993
- Two-time American Driver of the Year — 1987, 1994
- Four-time winner of the International Race of Champions — 1990, 1995, 1999, 2000
- Seven-time winner of the Goody's 300 Busch Series at Daytona (including five straight wins from 1990–1994)
- Daytona 500 Winner — 1998
- First American driver to receive the *Autosport* Gregor Grant Award
- First Winston Cup driver to drive at Suzuka Circuit, Japan

- Twelve-time winner of the 125-mile qualifying race at Daytona (including ten straight wins from 1990–1999)
- Named ESPY's "Driver of the Decade" (1990s)
- 2000 marked Dale's twenty-second full season on the NASCAR Winston Cup Circuit
- "Most Popular Driver" Award, 2001